. . . and Nick

by Emily Gore

illustrated by Leonid Gore

ATHENEUM BOOKS FOR YOUNG READERS
New York London Toronto Sydney New Delhi

To my dad.
I hope you like the flower
I grew up to be.
—E. G.

To my daughter,
whom I will always love
no matter what.
—L. G.

ATHENEUM BOOKS FOR YOUNG READERS
An imprint of Simon & Schuster Children's Publishing Division
1230 Avenue of the Americas, New York, New York 10020

Book design by Debra Sfestios-Conover
The text for this book is set in Blocky Fill.
The illustrations for this book are rendered in acrylic.
Manufactured in China
0315 SCP
First Edition
10 9 8 7 6 5 4 3 2 1
Library of Congress Cataloging-in-Publication Data
Gore, Leonid, author, illustrator.
And Nick / by Leonid Gore, with Emily Gore. — First edition.
pages cm
Summary: "There are four mice brothers: Rick, Mick, Vick . . . and Nick! Nick is the youngest, and
while his brothers each know exactly what they want, Nick is never quite sure. But he might be
waiting for the right moment to bloom."—Provided by publisher.
ISBN 978-1-4169-5506-1 (hardcover)
ISBN 978-1-4814-2623-7 (eBook)
[1. Brothers—Fiction. 2. Individuality—Fiction. 3. Mice—Fiction.] I. Gore, Emily, author. II. Title.
PZ7.G659993An 2015
[E]—dc23
2014021971

THERE were four little mice: Mick, Rick, Vick, and Nick.

They were brothers and looked very much alike, so much alike that their mother often could not tell them apart. For that reason, she brought them differently colored shirts to wear.

"I like the blue shirt. It is the color of the deep ocean and the clear sky," said Mick. "It is the color of adventure."

"I want the yellow shirt. It is the brightest," said Vick. "Like the color of a school bus."

"My favorite is the red one—the color of a fire engine. The color of bravery," said Rick.

The only shirt left for Nick was not as bright as Vick's yellow shirt, not as heroic as Rick's red shirt, and not as adventurous as Mick's blue one.

Nick's shirt was green—the color of spring leaves. And he liked it, too.

The brothers were very picky eaters.

Rick always chose
the red apple.

Vick liked cheese the most.

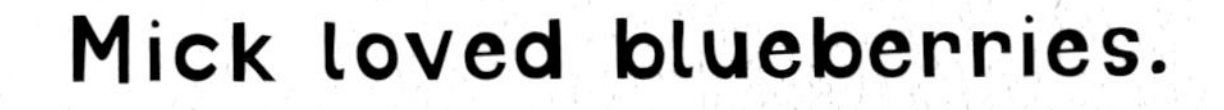

Mick loved blueberries.

Nick liked juicy red apples too . . . and cheese, and blueberries.

He liked them all and didn't know which one to choose.

So he decided to try a green salad. He'd heard it was healthy.

"I can sing very loud," Vick said. "When I grow up, I am going to be a famous singer."

"I am going to be an Olympic champion," said Rick. "I am really strong. I can lift a teddy bear, a train, and a sailboat all at once."

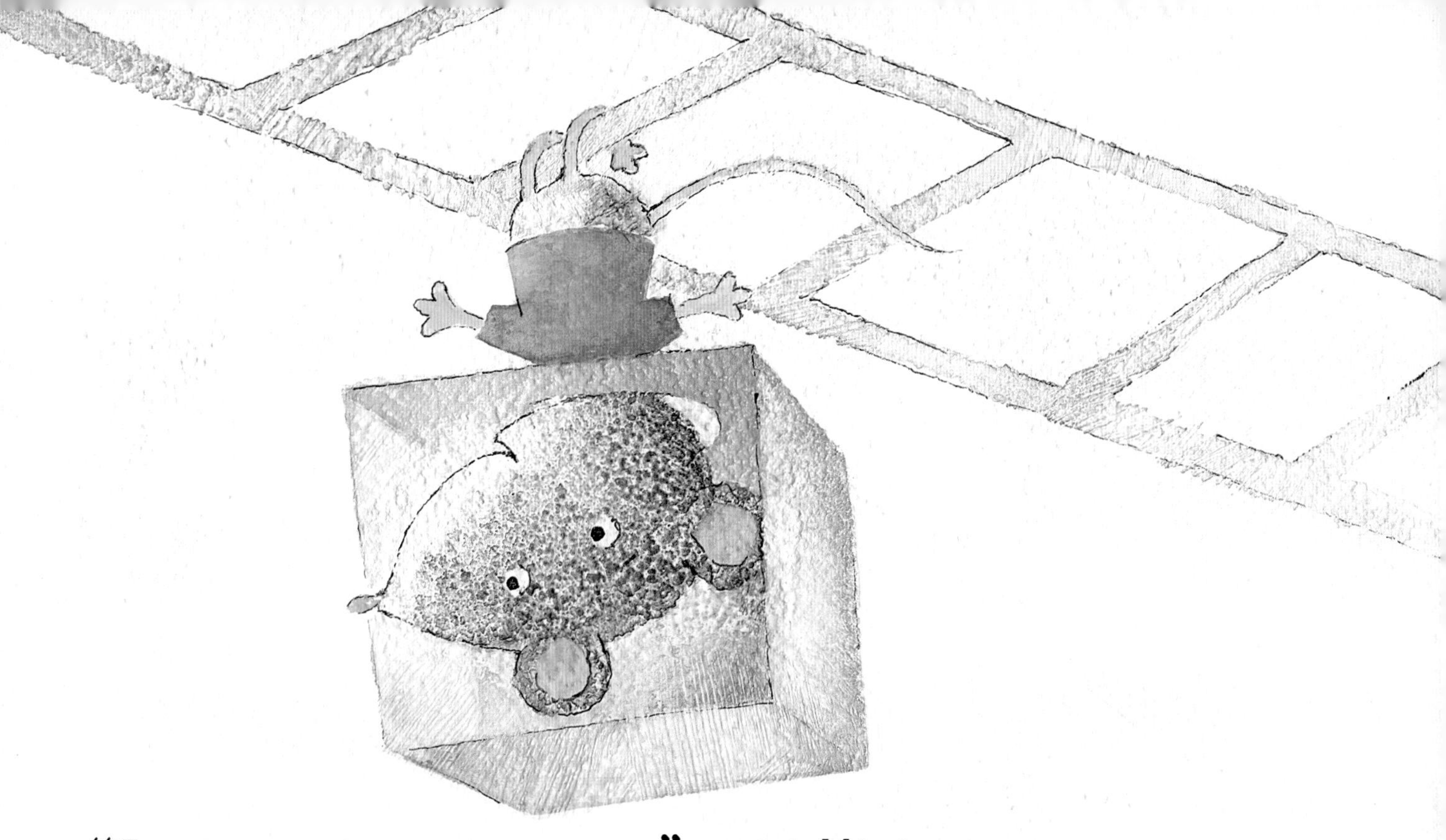

"I will be an astronaut," said Mick.
"I can hang upside down all day."

Nick liked to sing, he wanted to be strong, and he thought a flight to space could be very interesting. But he wasn't sure yet who he wanted to be.

One sunny afternoon, the four brothers decided to go to the meadow to gather flowers for Mommy.

Like all mice, they loved to ride fast.

Rick rode on his red bicycle,
Vick rode on his yellow bicycle,
Mick rode on his blue bicycle . . .

. . . and Nick tried his best to catch
up on his green tricycle.

The meadow was on the other side of the deep brook.

Mick ran fast across the bridge.
Vick ran even faster.
Rick ran the fastest . . .
. . . and Nick could not keep up with his brothers.

He could only think about the deep, deep brook down below.

Of course, Rick got to the meadow first.

"This beautiful red flower
will be mine," he claimed.

Mick said, "I want the
blue flower."

"I will take this yellow
one," said Vick.

When Nick finally arrived,
there were no flowers left for him.

Only a small green sprout.

"It is very small," remarked Rick.
"It is so green," laughed Mick.
"It is not special," said Vick.

Yes, it was not a real flower yet, but it looked so tender. Nick liked it.

"I hope Mommy will like this delicate sprout too," said Nick, and he took it home.

Rick proudly gave Mommy his red flower.

Vick handed her the yellow flower.

Mick presented her with the blue flower . . .

. . . and Nick gave Mommy his sprout.

Mommy put all the flowers and the sprout in her favorite vase, hugged all her sons, and said,

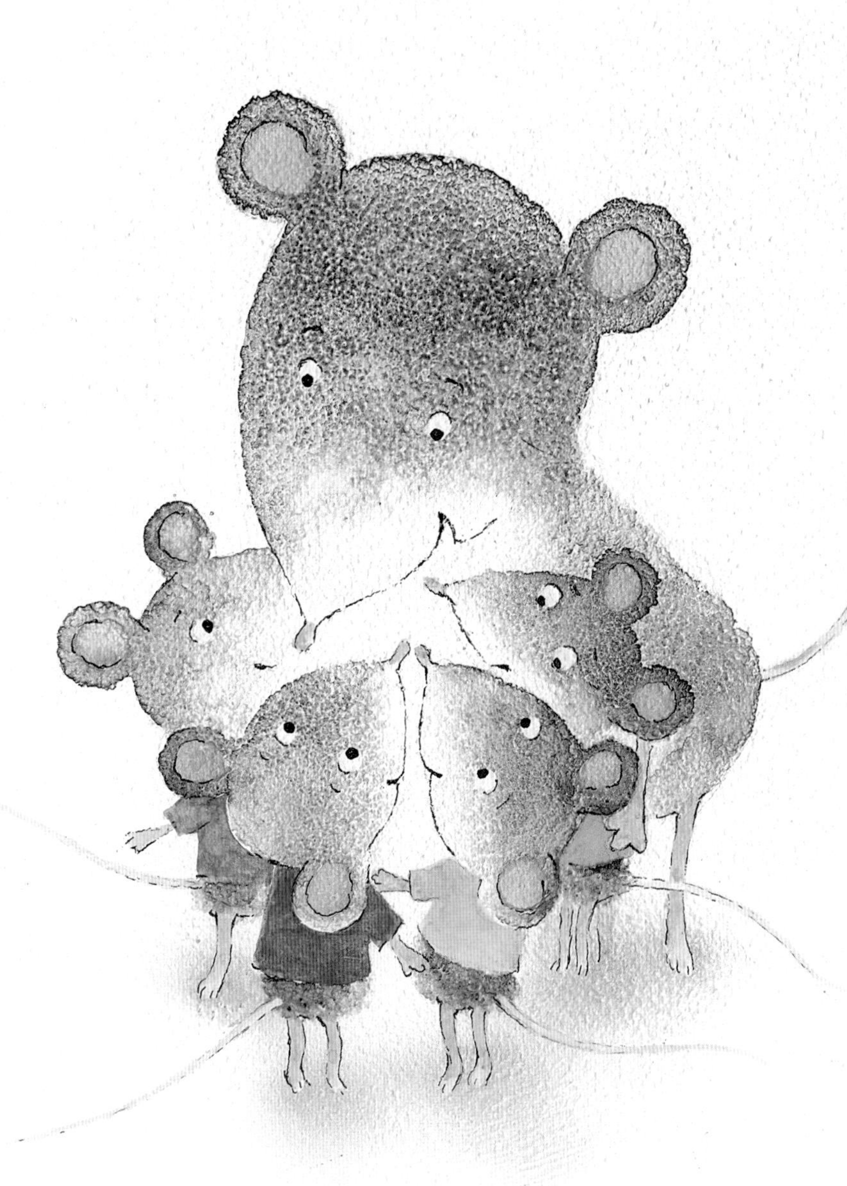

"I love you, Mick.

I love you, Rick.

I love you, Vick.

I love you, Nick.

I love you all very much."

When it came time to sleep, the four brothers kissed Mommy good night and went to their beds.

That night, Vick had a dream about being a famous singer.

Rick had a dream about being an Olympic champion.

Mick had a dream about being the first astronaut to land on Mars . . .

. . . and Nick could not sleep.

He could not stop thinking about the green sprout.

"Maybe my brothers are right. . . . It is not special."

If only it were as big, bright, and beautiful as the ones his brothers had found.

Early in the morning, before the sun came up,
Nick got on his tricycle to go to the meadow and
look for a new, colorful flower.

He ran across the bridge and tried not to think about the deep brook down below . . .

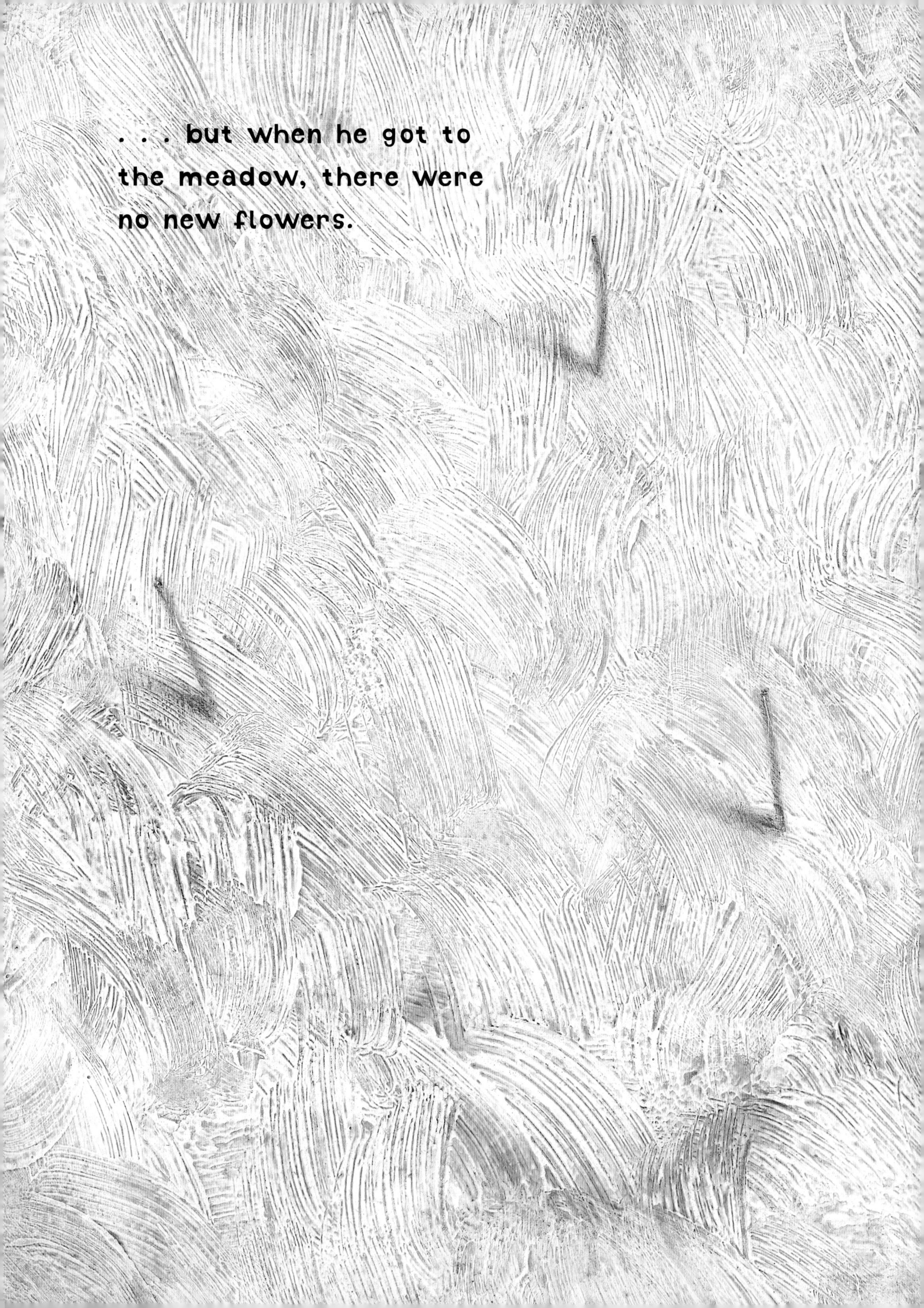

. . . but when he got to
the meadow, there were
no new flowers.

He looked everywhere—
there were no red
flowers like Rick's,
no yellow flowers like
Vick's, no blue flowers
like Mick's . . . not even
a small green sprout.

Nick headed back home. He was very, very sad.

But when he got
home, he could not
believe his eyes!

In the vase, instead of the small, fragile sprout, was the most magnificent flower he had ever seen.

"What an amazing flower!" exclaimed Mick.
"It is so unusual," said Rick.
"It is so beautiful," added Vick.
"Where did this wonderful flower come from?"
asked Mommy.

"It grew up from the small sprout I brought you yesterday," said Nick.

"What a special flower it is!" said Mommy.

"I guess it was a late bloomer."